THE ARCANE

2

THE ULTIMATE FATE

HRISHIKESH GOSWAMI

ISBN 978-93-5883-049-1
© HRISHIKESH GOSWAMI 2023

Published in India 2023 by Pencil

A brand of
One Point Six Technologies Pvt. Ltd.
Unit no. 26, Ground Floor, Building A1,
Wadala Truck Terminal Road,
Near Post Office, Antop Hill, Mumbai - 400037
E connect@thepencilapp.com
W www.thepencilapp.com

Author biography

(India Book of Records Holder for Poetry) (Creative Endeavour of The Month April 2021 by The Assam Tribune) (Recipient of India Prime Top 100 Author Award 2022) (Recipient of India Star Icon Award 2022)(Author of The Year 2021 Nominee) (Recipient of The Leading Attainers Award 2022) (Broadcasted in the Yuva Vani Programme of All India Radio) HRISHIKESH GOSWAMI is a Contemporary Naturalistic poet from Assam, India who specialises in writing about nature and realism coalescing fiction and non -fiction in a sophisticated blend. Author of The Poet's Words, The Secret: Nature Reveals, Poems for Poets, The Exegesis, 72 Haiku, 51st Tanka, The Sesquipedalian Notion, An

Aureate Opus of Quotes, Unveiling Beauty - Odes to the Extraordinary, The Arcane: The Adventures in Lavender, The Arcane: The Ultimate Fate, A Poet's Whim For Serendipity, How To Balance Coaching With School, How To Crack NEET-UG, A Fortuitous Odyssey, The Adventures of James Tony Morgan along with Co-Author of World Record Anthology Book – "Bilingual Aesthetics" and editor of the E-Poetry Anthology 'The Euphoric Verses from Soul' and the Literary Anthology 'Forest & Me' and 'The Idiosyncratic Mystery'.

Hrishikesh Goswami fell in love with writing from a fledgling age of 14 when he was at the 9th standard. Hrishikesh Goswami's poems have been featured in The Assam Tribune, Blue Lake Review, Indian Poetry Review, the Weaver Magazine, Poets India, Soul Connection brought up by Guwahati Grand Poetry Festival, Anthology Still I Rise brought out by Wingless Dreamer, Winter Poems Anthology brought out by Poets Choice. Hrishikesh Goswami has been highlighted by Media Houses such as India Saga, Daily hunt, Spot Latest, Fox Story India, Glamwist etc. Hrishikesh Goswami is also available in E platforms like Story mirror, Anchor, Spotify, Wattpad, Google Podcast, Apple Podcast, Breaker, Pocket Cast, Radio Public, All Poetry, Listen Notes, Wynk Music, Poetry Soup, Commaful, Hello Poetry, SoundCloud, Poem Hunter, Scribd, Vivlio, Angus & Robertson Store, Mondadori Store, Thalia, Indigo Books & Music, Kobo Inc., Apple Books etc. for his dear readers. Readers can find further information about the poet in Google and YouTube by typing "POET HRISHIKESH GOSWAMI " for the same.

Hrishikesh Goswami has cracked several competitive exams such as JEE Mains 2022, NEET-UG 2022, CUET 2022, IISER IAT 2022, KVPY 2022, AAU CET 2022, ASTU CEE 2022, IOQB-I and IOQC-I. He has been bestowed with Certificate of Commendation in Never Such Innocence International Poetry Contest, Certificate of Achievement from Asian Council for English Proficiency Test conducted under CAFLR norms, Semi-finalist of Under the Madness Magazine 2023 National Poetry Month competition, Certificate of Merit for Outstanding Performance in NationWide Mega Science Experiment Conducted by NCERT, VVM, VIBHA and Ministry of Education, Govt. of India, Editor's Choice Award in International Essay Writing Competition by Monomousumi and is recognised by World Record University, Career Development College London, Guwahati Grand Poetry Festival, WWF India, APJ. Abdul Kalam International Foundation, ASSIST WORLD RECORDS, PONDICHERRY BOOK OF RECORDS and Royal Commonwealth Society. He has been two times State Level Tae-kwon-do Champion, Gold Medallist of several National and International Competitive Exams and Olympiads, a KVPY Scholar, Winner of National School Level Essay Writing Contest conducted by Maulana Abul Kalam Azad Awards 2020, Grand Master of Mental Arithmetic-Senior A Whole Brain Development Program from Aloha (Abacus), Visharat in Hindustani Classical Music, Best Debater of PRARAMBH 2021 conducted by Nehru Group of Institutions, Kerala and Holder of Honourable Mention in several notable Poetry Competitions from around the World.

Apart from these Hrishikesh's poems have been critically analysed by Fruit Journal Manchester (UK), Acorn (A journal of contemporary haiku), The Leading Edge Magazine, BreakBread Magazine and has been published by The Assam Tribune's Horizon and Planet Young, NEZINE (An online magazine), Noverse Foundation & FoxGales Publishers, Poem hunter-The World's Poetry Archive, Pencil Publishers, Cultural Reverence (An International Digital Journal Of Art and Literature), Tech Touch Talk of Kolkata.

Hrishikesh Goswami's poems have been read by The Liminal Review, Poetry London, Talon Review, Appalachian Review, The Tether's End, Tears in the Fence Literary Journal, MASKS Literary Magazine, Ribbons, The Hopper (An environmental literary magazine), The West Trade Review, Split Rock Review, The Baltimore Review, Rollick Magazine, The Poetry Magazine, Chestnut Review, The Sun Magazine, The Society of Classical Poets, The Greensboro Review, The London Magazine, The Kenyon Review, The Adroit Journal, Washington Square Review, Wilderness House Literary Review and many more. Hrishikesh's haiku poem has been translated into Japanese and published in a traditional Japanese style literary anthology. A few of his poems have also been widely accepted in Poetry Circles and Forums.

CONTENTS

The Council.. 13

The Orb Promise 18

The Quest.. 22

The Dragon's Breath 26

The Prophecy Disclosed 31

The Awakening of the Celestial Powers............ 34

Into the Empire of Hallucinations 37

The Veiled City of Mysteries........................... 40

The Battle of the Elemental Forces 45

Whispers from the Whispering Isles................. 49

The Ricochet of Destiny.................................. 56

A Clash of Magic and Steel............................. 59

The Guardian's Scrutiny 61

The Psychic Rift 66

The Ultimate Fate 69

Acknowledgements

Dear Reader,

As I sit down to write this acknowledgement, I am occupied with a sense of gratitude and unpretentiousness. Writing a book is a solitary pursuit, but it is far from a solitary achievement. There are so many people who have backed this work in ways big and small, and I am extremely obligated to each and every one of them.

First and foremost, I want to thank my family and friends for their tireless assistance and corroboration. They have been there for me every step of the way, equipping me with the affection and support I needed to keep going when the going got tough!

I would take the time to express my onus to my editor and publisher for having confidence in this project and aiding to bring it to execution. Their skill, management, and feedback have been invaluable, and I could not have done this without them.

To the experts and sources who openhandedly pooled their time, knowledge, and insights with me, thank you for your munificence and readiness to share your expertise.

Your contributions have improved this work immeasurably.

Finally, to you, dear reader, thank you for taking the time to read this book. I hope that it edifies, inspires, and thrills you in ways that make a reformist impact on your life and the atmosphere around you.

With gratitude,
Hrishikesh Goswami

Introduction

In a world where obscurity lurks and vindictive influences threaten to shatter the fragile balance between virtuous and evil. Innocent and radiant Piper falls victim to the clutches of a seductive devil. Laven's heart compels him to take action. Bound by a profound and unyielding love, he sets forth on a treacherous expedition, braving the unknown and fronting ineffable perils to rescue his beloved. Driven by determination and fortified with unwavering resolve, Laven must navigate through a realm fraught with jeopardy and trickery. From perfidious landscapes to cunning adversaries, he must endure unimaginable destitutions and make sacrifices that will challenge his very essence.

As Laven's quest unfolds the line between reality and illusion blurs, the devil's enchantments threaten to devour him, while doubts and uncertainty cloud his path. The odds are stacked against him, and the outcome hangs in a precarious balance.

Will Laven emerge victorious from the clamps of the devil's seductive grip, or will he succumb to the perils that lie in wait?

In this gripping tale of love, sacrifice, and unconquerable will, join Laven on an unforgettable journey where the fate of his beloved hangs in the balance. Brace yourself for a rollercoaster ride of emotions, as danger and desire collide, and the true nature of heroism is put to the ultimate test.

The Council

Who might have even once thought in one of his or her wildest of the dreams that a mere fight of ego or a mere fight between two souls instigate a violent and ferocious clash between Gods and Demons (anti-Gods) of all ages.

As you might recall in 'The Arcane: The Adventures in Lavender' (i.e. Part 1) we saw Piper Forest, the daughter of the King of Mighty Wizards Kingdom, was abducted in a black horse by someone whose face was not visible to Laver, our protagonist. Although Laven followed them he was incapable to get hold of them as lots of confusion spells were casted upon him. Because of confusion spells and their deleterious effect Laven could not do anything but stood like a statue watching the brawny kidnapper riding his black horse with Piper deeper and deeper into the forest. And soon the horse and its rider became a dot in the far and after a few seconds completely vanished from Laven's field of vision!
I suppose you also remembered that this entire episode was silently observed by someone from the top! Do you remember? Yes, it was a wizard who was noiselessly observing the entire chain of events from his flying mat.

After a few hours, Laven found himself on a bed that once belonged to his father, the king of Lavender! Soon Laven realised what actually was happening...

Let me narrate you:

Quill was the antagonist in our first book and after her murder the kingdom of Lavender was freed from the dark spells that were casted on it by Quill and her acquaintance. Now the people of Lavender wanted Laven, the legal heir of King Hermit to take over the administration as the new King! That is why the ministers and well-wishers brought Laven back to the palace and endorsed their new King to take some respite in the same bed where once his father slept!

The room was too spacious and with the crack of dawn enough light entered the room through the panes of the royal windows. Laven was served red wine with some cookies that were arranged specially for him. After a few minutes, one old man knocked at the King's door. "Come in," said Laven. A six feet tall old man entered the room with his oversized clothing and nice and long white beard. "Your majesty, myself..." he continued, "You need not know my name for I was the chief of your father's council of ministers." Saying this the old man came two steps closer to Laven and continued, "As you might already be mindful that according to the policies espoused by our kingdom, you were supposed to be the next ruler of Lavender after your father's death but time was not suitable and so...Nevertheless I wanted to deliberate with you some of our future plans that would transform our Lavender and get back its lost glory." Laven got up from his comfy bed and requested the old man to continue. "Your majesty, may I ask you about your health right now, I mean to say are you ok?!" Laven didn't reply which indicated that he was not ok. After a short moment of ample silence the old man decided to move out of the room fearing that the king was not in a good position to answer his questions and might even curse him. This was when Laven spoke out, "Sir, I respect your loyalty towards my father and towards this kingdom of Lavender. Lavender was for such a long time under malevolent forces and so its administration was shattered into pieces. I am presently in grief!"

"What grief your majesty...you are the King! King of this beautiful kingdom of Lavender."said the minister. "I am deeply shaken with the death of my mother, father, Grand, Boha. Moreover I was not able to protect Piper Forest, her father might be very dismayed in heaven right now for I was not able to keep up the promise I made to him. And above all, I killed Quill with deceit" replied Laven.

"Your majesty, what should we do with Quill's dead body? Should we put it into public exhibition for she was a traitor!"

enquired the minister to which Laven replied in negative.

Laven left his room along with the old man following him and pushed into the planning room. He called for a conference with the important ministers and stakeholders of the kingdom. In the meeting Laven outlined some of his future moves. They were:

1. Fortify Lavender's present border with magical walls which will be impervious to malevolent forces.

2. Rearm his troops and recruit some new players into his army.

3. Improve the existing relations of Lavender with the neighbouring kingdoms.

4. Build a few more magic schools so that Lavender's children and teenagers could learn magic and use it for social good.

5. Laven would go for an expedition.

All the important ministers accepted the proposal except the last one. They didn't want to lose one of their beloved kings to die in a mere expedition. Moreover Lavender needs some sort of stability for it to recover from such trauma and angst.
Also Laven didn't have a legal heir so if something happens to Laven, Lavender would go headless.
Laven understood the insecurities of his ministers and assured them that he would first accomplish the first four goals and then go out for his expedition.
After a heated debate amongst the ministers and stakeholders finally the house came to the conclusion that they would go with Laven's current proposal.

Soon the construction works began and recruitment camps were set up nearly in every corner of the kingdom. Lavender was beautified with flowers, silver and gold.

Tourists came from far off places to admire the prettiness and serenity of this kingdom.Laven regularly passed policies that would strengthen the kingdom and help it recover fast from its bloody past. Soon Lavender's foreign relationship upgraded several fold but unfortunately the old man, the chief, died because of massive internal bleeding. Perhaps he had a peptic ulcer. Laven didn't allow construction works to slow down but now the kingdom was slowly running out of funds. Laven turned his attention to exports and liberalised the stringent policies.

Countrymen declared Laven as the best king history has ever seen. But something was constantly disturbing Laven. His mental state was not serene as his physical state was. He was trying to figure out the abductor of Piper Forest. And for this purpose he had appointed five spies in the neighbouring kingdoms who reported him weekly.

The Orb Promise

Few months went happily and prosperity prevailed almost everywhere in Lavender. The King was satisfied and so was his council. The actors acted, painters painted, singers sang and dancers danced blissfully without any fear. Gods from heaven were observing Laven's selfless deeds and blessing him a long and productive life.

One fine day, the wind was blowing unusually and its roar was clearly falling in Laven's ears who was sitting up straight in his bedroom chair looking at the open window that had a few potted plants and a liana by its side. The rose pink curtain gave way to the wind that moisturised Laven's skin. It also sucked the sweat which occasionally appeared when Laven got excited or nervous. Laven was not able to find a single clue to proceed for his fifth target i.e. his expedition.

This was when the wind speed increased several folds and a red mat was spotted by Laven that was hanging outside the window. He stood up quickly from his statue position and ran like anything towards the window and got a good grip over that mat. With full might he pulled that mat inside his room and along with it came a wizard!

Astonished Laven didn't speak a word. The wizard broke the silence by giggling like a monkey and said, "My son, I know where Piper is... rather I should say I know who took Piper from you." Laven didn't believe that old wizard at one go but soon gave up when the wizard narrated the entire episode which was as exact as a crystal. Laven asked the wizard to tell him about the whereabouts of Piper and in return promised him a position in the royal council. The wizard was not greedy nor was he in a position of holding power at least at this age. He said, "Boy, I can't tell you where Piper is now but I can tell you who abducted Piper." The guards standing outside Laven's room heard the humming of the wizard and quickly entered the room to protect their king from danger (if any). Laven indicated to them with his hand that everything was well and there was nothing to worry about. The wizard sat on the floor and Laven also accompanied him. "My dear wizard, where were you all these days? Why didn't you report me? Are you scared of something?"

The wizard scratched his beard and took out his wand. He drew some shapes in the air and brought a map like thing from thin air. He then laid the map over the floor," This map is of heaven! I found this in my library, pressed between two pages of an old dusty book. This map gives us some information which I have tried to figure out all these days. Now that I have deciphered most of the meanings I want to share them with you. But before that promise me that you will get me that orb." said the wizard indicating towards a small circle in the map. The circle was marked over a tower-like structure and there was simply nothing else in the map except a few letters inscribed here and there.

"I will surely get you that orb or whatever that is but just tell me one thing why are you helping me?! I met you for the very first time and I don't even know your name."said Laven who was curious to know about this sorcerous person. "My name is Ethan Stormrider, and I was the most beloved student of Grand. Grand was my godfather and when he died I wept a lot. I promised myself that I would punish the killer but now that you have already killed her I want to help you out. And let me tell you that I am not going to answer any of your questions now because my question answering limit is over. So kindly don't ask me any more questions and just listen to me closely."said the old wizard.

Laven wanted to ask a few more questions to this man especially about that orb but if he would ask there was a high chance that this old man would leave his room through the window and never return. So it was prudent for him not to ask.

"Your friend, Piper Forest was abducted by a very strong devil named Gabriel Thornheart (GT). GT is backed by demons and also by some divine forces. His supernatural abilities can defy science as well as magic. His lust is very potent and he can cross any limits towards accomplishing the same. I can very well say arcate that your friend, Piper Forest must be undergoing tough times in GT's regime. You must leave at once to defend her from that lustful creature!"stammered the old wizard. Very soon the wizard broke into tears and his blood pressure fell drastically.

Laven called for the royal doctors and somehow revitalised Ethan. According to a doctor, Ethan is suffering from a very deep grief. For a few days the doors of Laven's room remained open to visitors who came to enquire about Ethan's health condition. From these people Laven came to know that Ethan's daughter was also abducted by GT a few years ago. An apprehensive Laven made up his mind to start his expedition. He was directed to move eastward and halt at a village where he would meet Felix Midnight, a localite who had a potency of guiding Laven further.

The Quest

Laven, Nova Whitethorn (Laven's personal bodyguard), Isolde Moonstone (Laven's personal assistant) and Asher Winterbourne (Army chief) sat together in the planning room one evening and deliberated over their course of action. The expedition team would consist of

1. This four
2. Two elite warriors
3. Few flying horses
4. One healing unicorn
5. Three helpers

The team planned their journey the very next morning eastwards. The flying horses were newly trained and so were a bit difficult to harness.

Next morning the weather was pleasant and the sun was shining luminously over the lakes and rivers of Lavender. The expedition team started off from the royal palace and after flying for four hours halted on top of a hill. They had already traversed Lavender's magic wall and were now in foreign territory. Nova kept a keen eye on his master's security while the two elite warriors escorted the team.

Laven ordered the helpers to refill their wine glasses and after a few minutes, the team continued eastwards. Below them were vast stretches of forest, lake, river and low mountains. The team was flying without any struggle except for facing a few gusts of strong winds. It was almost noon when Laven ordered the team to halt for lunch. They landed over a low hill and had a very good lunch. Any layman would easily identify them as royals with their dress code. Laven was wearing a golden armour while the others wore armours made out of silver. The elite warriors had their own unique style of dressing.

After lunch the team was tired and didn't fly anymore. That night was well spent with lots of food, wine and juice. Next morning the team started further eastward and reached an enchanted village. The people here were very caring and hospitable to their royal guests. The chief of the village was also a simple man. He offered that night's stay to the visitors and promised them full security. Laven and his team halted there for the night. They also relished fresh juice, music, dance and poetry there.

Little did Laven and his team realise that these villagers were actually his foes. The next morning, the team was astonished to find not a single gold coin. All their food and wine was confiscated and the villagers deserted the village. What remained were the abandoned houses and a few elderly people of the village who said that the youth of the village had started a new business of stealing visitors of their gold and food material. Laven was very angry but didn't react as he understood the desperate need of time. He had already wasted most of his time in pleasure and fun and now time was moving very fast. It would be very bad if something happens to Piper only because of negligence and procrastination of the King of Lavender.

The team hurriedly got ready and flew towards east for another few hours when they came across another village amidst the desert. Laven didn't halt and continued his expedition thinking that such a small village would not house such a significant person, a person who was so important for the King of Lavender.

After flying the whole day Laven didn't progress much in finding the village which he was supposed to so he ordered the team to take a U-turn. Upon reaching that very small village which Laven once neglected, the team landed. The elite warriors made way for their King and Laven who was very hungry and tired by now wanting the help of the villagers. The villagers here were poor and didn't have much to help the King out. Laven had to sleep that night with little food. Next morning, Laven freshened himself up and wore a dress which was offered to him with love by a poor villager. "Why is this village so lightly populated?"asked Laven to which an unexpected answer came,"This village was not like this a few months ago but a notorious dragon and its master invaded us and took away the lot we had. Legends say that the dragon and its master reside somewhere far away in a hill and occasionally appear to loot villages and abduct people, especially teen girls! Laven was curious to know about the dragon and its owner and so he called for a meeting of the villagers. That morning the village people who were a few hundred in number congregated below a huge tree. Laven shouted,"Can anyone give me the exact whereabouts of the dragon and its master! I will promise you that I will kill it and bring back your girls."

No one opened his or her mouth. Laven understood that it was of little worth trying to help these people as they barely speak about the dragon. Maybe they are very petrified of something or...

One very old man stepped forward and said,"Your majesty, the great King of Lavender, I am Felix Midnight and I have the command to help you out in this expedition; however I don't know much about the dragon you are chatting about." "Please continue,"cried Laven. "For that you have to come to my room, your majesty." said Midnight.

Laven followed Felix to his room which was well lit and pleasingly ventilated. Something was unusual about Felix. He always kept a critical smile on his face and his eyes sometimes turned colourful as noticed by Laven. That evening, when Laven and Felix sat on the floor of Felix's hut, Laven felt the aura of Grand! He became nostalgic about the days when Grand used to sit by his side and tell Laven stories of far off land. Grand's presence was enough for a miserable and dejected Laven to break into bouts of laughter.

"Listen my son..." tenderly started the old man.

The Dragon's Breath

"Time is very unsuitable for you. This is the time when Zephyrus, the God of Dark vigour awakes from slumber and blesses his devotees with mammoth power. In such a status quo GT will become super commanding and it will be unmanageable for you and your magical influences to capture him and get Piper out of danger. The journey is challenging and there seems no assurance that you will return alive. It will be better if you take your path back to Lavender and relish a joyful King's life there. That's an old man's advice."

"Sir, I have no idea regarding Gods and Demons. I know only one thing and that is combat. I will fight till my last breath. No God or Demon can thwart me from rescuing Piper."declared Laven.

"Your determination is nuanced by the desperate needs of nature. Young people like you are standing up to combat GT and castigate him for all of his wrong deeds but none have thrived so far at least in my knowledge."Felix continued,"You are a King and I will not avert you from doing anything whether right or wrong but remember one thing Piper needs you."

The old man's statements were quite contradictory. He tries to coax Laven to not go further but at the same time encourages him to do so. What does this man actually want?

Next morning Laven was dusting his sword and spear as if he was getting prepared for a duel. "At last you have decided to go,"said the old man observing Laven's actions. "Now that you have already decided let me not demoralise you but keep one thing in mind, Gods are with GT!!"said Felix. "Shut up! Gods, Demons and all that. You are such a confusing old man. What do you actually want? Should I go or not?! Why don't you make your statements clear?"bellowed Laven.

The old man said that he is apprehensive of the upcoming shadowy nights and at the same time optimistic about the illuminating Sun. It so happened that amidst the conversation news came that the dragon had been spotted! Laven swiftly tied the laces of his boots and went off to kill it. It was a royal Rage of Quill (hope you remember from the previous book). In a realm of soaring mountains and lush valleys, Laven found himself face to face with a legendary, deadly dragon. The dragon's scales gleamed with an obsidian sheen, its fiery breath billowing with an intimidating force. Undeterred by fear, Laven steeled his resolve, for he knew the fate of his village rested upon his shoulders.

The battle commenced as Laven deftly dodged a searing stream of flames, his nimble feet propelling him away from certain peril. With a flick of his wrist, he unsheathed a gleaming silver sword, its blade shimmering in the sunlight. Laven's heart pounded with determination as he lunged forward, slashing at the dragon's scaly hide with every ounce of strength he possessed.

The dragon roared in fury, releasing a mighty swipe of its colossal claw. Laven promptly rolled to the side, narrowly evading the monstrous attack. Taking advantage of the dragon's momentary vulnerability, Laven sprang back to his feet, his sword poised to strike. With a resolute cry, he delivered a lightning-fast series of slashes, aiming for the creature's vulnerable spots.

Though the dragon's size and strength were overwhelming, Laven relied on his agility and wit. He darted beneath the dragon's colossal frame, leaping and rolling between its towering legs with incredible speed. The dragon's tail whipped through the air, but Laven managed to duck and weave, narrowly escaping its bone-crushing blows. Summoning his courage, Laven climbed upon the dragon's back, clutching tightly to its formidable scales. With a swift motion, he buried his sword deep into the dragon's neck, piercing its impenetrable armour. The dragon roared in agony, thrashing wildly in an attempt to dislodge its determined adversary.

Unyielding, Laven clung to the dragon's back, his grip unshaken. He dug his heels into the creature's sides, urging it toward the edge of a nearby cliff. As the dragon neared the precipice, Laven unleashed a final burst of strength, guiding the colossal beast over the edge. The dragon plummeted into the abyss, its deafening roar fading into the distance.

Laven stood victorious, his chest heaving with exertion and triumph. With his head held high, Laven returned to his village, forever etched in their hearts as the courageous young warrior who had vanquished the mighty dragon and brought peace to their land. After that the owner was pitilessly beaten up by the villagers and he had to convey them about the whereabouts of the teen girls. All these girls were circulated to GT! So now the need to find and kill GT became desperate in the mind of Laven.

The old man came to Laven and said,"You will need the blessings of Goddess Astralyn."

"Who is goddess Astralyn and where will I find her?"asked Laven. "Goddess can't be found son! You will have to please her with your utmost commitment, devotion and unwavering determination! You will find her temple over a hill towards the South-west of this village not very far away."replied the old Felix.

Laven wanted to know more about Gods and Goddesses and so he persuaded Felix to tell him further before he actually took any step further. Gradually and progressively Laven was getting nervous of the powers of Gods! Observing the curiosity of the King, the old man got up and advanced towards his kitchen to get a glass of warm water for himself as he knew that a long history will have to be repeated to transmute a novice King into a matured one!

After a few minutes the old man returned and resumed. "My boy, let me tell you about the Gods and Goddess who will now largely decide the success or failure of your expedition! Open your eyes, ears and shut your mouth for the time being!!"cried Felix.

The Prophecy Disclosed

"This is the story not of man. When God Morokar was the King of Heaven. He was an inordinate administrator and under his regime demons dared not to touch the doors of Heaven. But Morokar had a weakness which was known only to God Nexus who was a shrewd mind. He was Morokar's nephew and was not a very generous one. Nexus knew that the only way to get the throne of Heaven was by eliminating his uncle Morokar!

Morokar had a son and a daughter named Zephyrus and Astralyn respectively. But both of them always kept quarrelling over trivial things and slowly and steadily seeds of hostility were sown in between these two with Nexus as catalyst! It is normally said that Nexus overheard a conversation between Morokar and his wife Aurora in which Morokar was describing to her how he became the King of Heaven and what was the vital link which kept reinforcing and revitalising him as the King!

Nexus used his clever mind to manipulate Zephyrus that time has arrived when he (Zephyrus) and not Morokar needs to control Heaven. Zephyrus, thinking Nexus to be a well-wisher followed the path shown to him by Nexus. It is said that Zephyrus made Nexus his teacher and believed him more than anyone in the entire Heaven.

One day, when essential deliberations were going on between the key controllers of Heaven, Zephyrus interrupted the discussion which offended his father Morokar and Morokar stood up and yelled at Zephyrus who in turn shouted back at his father. Nexus was adoring the whole episode from a distance. Astralyn arrived at the scene only to make it worse. She screamed at Zephyrus for not being cooperative with his father and for not following the rules of Heaven. She announced that Zephyrus, her brother, was not adept of running Heavenly matters and should be sent to Hell! Hearing these forbidding words from his sister's mouth, Zephyrus took out his double headed axe and ran like a bull towards Astralyn in order to harm her! Seeing this violence and fearing any future impairment, Morokar cursed both his son and daughter that they both will not be able to co-exist together in any one place for more than the time required by a feather to reach the ground when released from the neck level of Aurora on Earth! The reason behind choosing this time as great scholars say is that this much time will not be sufficient for either of them to totally annihilate the other!

As a result of this curse, Nexus was unsuccessful in his plan of dethroning the King as the King's power derives from the survival of both his Son and Daughter and this is why he was especially watchful about the simultaneous existence of both!"said Felix.

After narrating this much the old man took a deep breath and relaxed. Laven was in deep thought. He was thinking how the voracity for power debases the mind of even Gods. In such a scenario, struggling for power amongst people like them was quite acceptable! After a long pause Felix sustained,"Gods and Goddess differ from us in a lot of ways; we can't become Gods or Goddess merely by acquiring a lot of land or a lot of power! Many warriors forget this thing and end up comparing themselves to Gods! We ought not to challenge God ourselves because that could be disastrous and that was why I was averting you from proceeding further with your expedition!"

"But now that you have decided to go, I have no other alternative than to show you that path for I too need a thing, the Orb!!"whispered the old man deeply.

Laven now was eager to visit the temple of Astralyn and worship her and asked Felix if he would like to join the expedition to which the old man replied in affirmative.

Now that one more member joined the expedition the team was compelled to leave their flying horses there in the village and undergo the rest of the journey on foot.

The Awakening of the Celestial Powers

Next morning was very sunny and the sun was as bright as the hopes within Laven who was ascending up the hill towards the temple of Astralyn. It was at the topmost point of the hill and the entire desert was visible from there. Wind speed was high here and scaling was a bit difficult. Trees were plenty but the rocky terrain made it challenging for devotees to move up and down regularly. Nevertheless Laven reached the gate of the temple and offered his prayer to Astralyn. He meditated outside the temple below a very old tree for a few hours and before returning made sure that the temple premises were clean and secured. He continued his prayer for almost a week when one day something unexpected happened.

It so happened that Laven was serenely seated below the same old tree when the wind speed increased by several times and sounds of birds became very strong. Laven could also hear the sound produced by the rubbing of the leaves. He looked all around for anything extraordinary but in vain. Similar events sustained for a few more days and made Laven curious.

One fine day, it rained profoundly; the sky was almost black with dark thick clouds obstructing the rays of the Sun. This was when a golden aura was spotted by Laven and a voice came from somewhere which said-"Laven Warlock, Astralyn is pleased with your devotion and I am willing to help you out if you need any...! Don't hesitate my son, I will protect you!" Laven was totally dumbfounded. He never expected this to occur in the wildest of his dreams. He even confirmed by touching his elbows and knees. After a protracted period of silence he opened his mouth fearing that any unnecessary word if uttered could be very fatal. He said slowly,"It's my pleasure to serve the great Gods and Goddesses. I don't need any sort of help right now!"

Astralyn said,"Are you sure you don't need my help to fight Gabriel Thornheart?!"

Again after a protracted period of silence Laven said,"Hey Goddess, how do I request your help! I am a novice and I have little knowledge regarding these things."

Astralyn said,"Fear not! I will be there when you will be requiring my help the most...!" Saying this the aura disappeared into thin air and ordinary conditions resumed which encompassed ordinary wind speed, temperature and rattle. Laven after concluding his regular service in the temple returned with a broad smile of satisfaction. Felix recognized his smile and reverted back with an even broader smile.

The next day, Felix, Laven, Nova and all the other members of the team deliberated over their forthcoming journey. Felix exhibited them a map and explained it to them in simple terms.

He said," Now we need to change our direction to North from East. We will be scaling towards the Northern mountains, and after scaling them we will enter into the Serenity Glen and then into these Whispering Isles..."

The team headed towards the North with Felix as a new team mate. Everyone was excited to hear stories that Felix generally used to narrate when he saw the youth showing signs of boredom. The mountains were steep and the paths were tapered, somehow allowing a person to pass by. After walking for a few hours they came across three teenage boys who were returning from their hunt. They crossed by Laven and his team and one of them whispered something into the ear of an elite warrior. The elite warrior reported it to Laven's personal bodyguard who then reported it to Laven," Your majesty, according to these boys, Vorka is out!" Felix overheard them and said,"Ah! Vorka is a stunning creature that inhabits this mountain. It can be fatal if you go too close to it."

Laven paid little attention to Felix and continued marching. After about half an hour of continuous marching the team was forcefully stopped by the Vorka. It was enormous but not violent. Laven first tried to negotiate but when negotiation failed he had to take to arms. The two elites were asked to attack the Vorka from its flanks. But little did he expect the outcome. The Vorka striked one elite with its long claw and bit the other. The one that was bitten died immediately for its venom contains neurotoxin. The one who was injured remained unconscious. Laven's personal bodyguard released a super powerful fire arrow and burned one half of the creature. After a few minutes the creature collapsed spontaneously due to excessive fluid loss. The injured elite finally recovered with sufficient aid and the team which now had one member less continued further.

Into the Empire of Hallucinations

After two days of exhaustive trekking the Northern mountains were overcome by the team. They lost one member of the team and one was wounded. Felix continued to narrate stories so as to motivate everyone. Everyone also encouraged themselves by looking at each other. Finally Serenity Glen was reached. Here they saw a magic line spread throughout. Felix said that magic would no longer work once they cross this magic line. According to him it is the first line of defence for Gabriel Thornheart. Laven didn't hesitate to cross the line although the other members of his team did. People of Lavender are well acquainted with the use of magic for day to day purposes and also for self-defence. Adapting to a non-magic environment was totally novel for them. They started to feel a bit helpless. Physical and mental valour are the only weapons which they now possess. Serenity Glen was an overwhelming place which was not touched much by travellers as they feared to cross the magic line. Laven drank a lot of water as he was dehydrated during the journey. Felix requested him to take a break but Laven didn't pay courtesy. He kept on marching for time was less and Piper's life might be in danger.

That night a devastating thunderstorm hit the team. Most of their food was wasted and soon there was a massive flood. The team somehow swam to a high land and collected some fresh fruits and berries but these were not fit for consumption and one of the helpers died by consuming it. After travelling some more distance the land splitted into two and a large trough developed. Felix fell into it but he hastily grabbed a dried branch of a tree and was later evacuated from there. But this was not the happy ending; troubles were yet to come. By this time Gabriel Thornheart was already informed about a team that was hurriedly progressing towards his kingdom. Gabriel kept a close eye on the activities and behaviour of Laven and others. He sent for a succubus that has never failed to please Gabriel in the past and was very loyal to him.

That night was particular because Laven had to dodge the attack of this succubus but Laven was not aware of it.

Next morning it was seen that Asher Winterbourne, the chief of the Lavendorian army was found dead. He was killed by cyanide poisoning as declared by Felix who had seen such kinds of deaths in his village earlier. Asher Winterbourne's dressing showed that most probably he was visited by a succubus the previous night! Now it was very clear to Laven that Gabriel is trying to kill all the members of his team including him so the time has come that they become cautious about each and every step they put forward!

It was here in Serenity Glen that the road divided into two. One which headed towards the Whispering Isles and the other to The Great Tower of Nexus. Laven wanted to take the first one but Felix opposed his decision for Felix wanted the Orb that was securely kept inside the Tower of Nexus. Laven also had promised Ethan Stormrider that he would get the Orb for him. After a protracted debate, the team agreed to take the second route towards the Great Tower of Nexus.

Laven asked Felix about the Orb to which he said that only wizards know about it that too the veteran ones so it was not necessary for Laven to know about it in great detail. However when Nova also pressed for the explanation along with Laven, Felix had to unveil the secret.

"The Orb"he said,"is a very powerful celestial element and its energy is required by any wizard who is willing to become immortal or for that matter undefeatable. After soaking the power from the Orb the Orb shall get destroyed by itself but Gods don't want wizards of Earth to become immortal because then these wizards will create havoc in Heaven. Morokar has handed the task of protection of Orb to Nexus and so Nexus built a legendary tower which is now known as The Great Tower of Nexus. It is a massive one and also quite impressive!"

After hearing this, Laven's personal assistant cried,"Mr.Felix, are you a wizard?!" To this the old man replied,"I was one until we crossed that magic line but now I am nothing more than a mere accumulation of flesh and bones with some blood!"

Laven wanted to have a sight of this famous tower but he was not willing to get inside it and get the Orb for he by this time already understood the supremacies and anger of Gods. He especially was apprehensive of God Nexus who was impish and shrewd. But since he already made a promise he now had no other way than to get the Orb!

The Veiled City of Mysteries

The temperature was leisurely escalating and so was humidity. Hums and cries of mythical animals were approaching from a distance. The team was getting thrilled to view the Tower of Nexus. Felix told them to become vigilant of their immediate surroundings because anything can happen. The road was not well laid and very few people actually passed by this one. Rivers of some colourful substance was spotted by the helpers but they didn't go close to it fearing curse from the God Nexus. Finally the team was thoroughly tired of walking and sat down for a few minutes. They wanted water as heat and moisture were very oppressive. It was even fierier than the hottest day of summer. Felix recapped them that nothing here was safe to touch and so drinking or eating anything here was out of question. Soon the team saw a very very old person heading towards them. He was wearing a unique chain around his neck and he had a short beard. His eyes were barely open and his ears were not clearly visible because of his huge heap of hoary hair. His skin was too loose and he had a walking stick on one hand and a book on the other. The old man neared Laven's personal assistant Isolde and requested him to hold his book for a second. A tired Isolde somehow loses his grip and the book falls on his boots. The old man suddenly grew so annoyed that he threw his stick into the air and turned it into a perilous sword which he immediately thrusted into Isolde's belly and killed that innocent soul. Laven quickly took out his own sword and unglued the old man's head from his body. The head fell on the road and soon disappeared. Felix picked up the book but it spontaneously caught fire and the sword which the old man thrusted into Isolde's abdomen also vanished into thin air. Laven was mad and so were the others. But Felix knew what was actually going on but he didn't say a word. The squad moved ahead and now with one member less. There was fear in the heart but Laven didn't express it only to keep his team motivated and kept moving.

Soon it was almost dark and started to drizzle. Laven felt as if Astralyn was present around him. He got inspired to achieve his ultimate goal. This was when another old man was walking in the same way as the first one was. He too had a book and a stick. He approached the team and gave one of the helpers his book to hold but this time the helper held the book as if it was a glass showpiece. The old man kept one end of his stick over the helper's chest and soon it turned into a long knife and went through the heart of that helper. Laven again took out his sword but this time the old man dodged. He gave a crooked smile and said,"Laven of Lavender, you are too selfish. You think only about that Piper and these old wizards. You have forgotten your kingdom and its people. Go back to your home and my master shall spare you."

Laven was about to do one more attack when someone held his hand from behind. Laven tried but could not free his wrist. He turned back and saw Nova who was nodding his head side to side indicating his master not to do so. Laven was surprised but slowly he reduced the tone of the extensors of his right hand and the old man vanished once again. Nova said that he saw the reflection of his father in that old man's face and so he stopped...

Felix was perplexed and didn't say a word. Laven too was very jumbled and closed his eyes as if trying to communicate with his Goddess. Soon the shady clouds gave off and what was divulged in front of the team was....

A huge black tower surrounded by mythical animals and below it ran a river not of water but of noxious elements. The fumes of these chemicals developed clouds of various colours that partially covered the entrance of the tower. The sky was turning dark as night was on its way. Temperature was still very high and the pillars in the ground were very unpolished. The tower's architecture was very unique and differed from the common architectural designs prepared by man. Laven was mystified to see a sharp ray of light getting emitted from within the tower and drifting upwards towards the sky. Just a few feet above the highest point of the tower was a glowing disc much like a miniature Sun. He kept on watching that unusual scene for a long time when Nova brought him his much-loved bow and arrow. Felix directed Laven to target that disc for it was the reflection of the Orb that was securely placed inside one of the secret rooms of the tower. Laven did so. Soon the disc started to emit strong waves of heat and light that made visibility very low. Laven and his team dashed towards the slab which was the only way to cross the river. They did cross the slab but the mythical animals were waiting on this side of the river to welcome the new guest. A creature that seemed like a mixture of lion and zebra leaped on Felix and scratched his chest. It then leaped on Laven but before it could do any harm, Nova pierced its abdomen with a long spear. Laven unconstrained another arrow towards the dragon that was hovering over the tower and soon the dragon landed on the ground and turned anything that came into its way into ashes. The elite fought courageously with the dragon and sliced off both its wings. After fighting with Laven's arrow in its breast and without its wings the dragon finally collapsed. Nova also killed the wolf-like beast that was trying to hurt one of the helpers. Laven pushed through the door of the Tower of Nexus and climbed up its spiral staircase to reach the top storey. But before he reached there he heard Nova scream from the ground floor and Laven took his way back to the ground floor. Felix on the other hand went upstairs via a different route. In a store room beside the main entrance Laven discovered Nova's dead body with a slitted neck! He died due to excessive blood loss. Most probably someone quietly got hold of Nova from his back and inserted a sharp knife…! Laven went across most of the rooms to find that nasty killer but in vain. Soon Felix cried,"Lavender's king please be here…I have something to show you!" Laven again went upstairs and Felix told him that he has found out the secret room where the Orb is placed! Both of them heroically dashed for the Orb. Laven broke the door of the room but Orb was not inside. This was when the ambience of the room changed drastically. Heavenly music was heard by both of them inside the room. The room's door locked automatically behind them and the windows unbolted wide. An aura of heavenly light brightened the dusky place and soon a terrific laughter was heard. "Some smell in the air"Laven said,"A smell I never got before!". "It is a unique smell indeed!"added Felix who was terrified with that sound of laughter. "Who is here, come in front and fight me!"cried Laven. "Brave Laven Warlock! How are you?" said a voice which was very childish. "I wasn't expecting you here at this point of time until you killed me by detaching my head from my body!"said a very deep voice as if a very old man was saying. Laven and Felix roamed across the room to find out who actually was playing jokes with them but that found none. At one point of time Felix got frustrated and decided to leave that place when someone abruptly appeared in front of him and pushed him out of the window with a jerk. The old Felix fell from the biggest window of the top storey and landed in the river of chemicals which blissfully separated his body from soul! Laven went running near the window when he heard Felix's scream for help. Laven turned his face towards the creature who pushed Felix into the river of death and was flabbergasted! Nexus it was.

Nexus was holding the Orb in his hand and laughing like anything. After a protracted period of laughter he finally spoke out in a ferocious voice, "Laven Warlock you are not a wizard and therefore you have no ambition for this Orb. You only need Piper and one who actually needed this Orb is dead so let this Orb stay with its protector and you go your way…!" Saying so the God disappeared into thin air and the ambience turned back into originality. The place which was so hot and humid slowly turned into a gorgeous forest with sufficient greenery and zephyr blew gratefully across the green landscape. The tall tower slowly started disintegrating into fragments and the river of chemicals turned into a lovely river of tranquil water.

The Battle of the Elemental Forces

Laven quickly ran out of the tower and met his team members who were waiting outside for him. They asked in chorus,"Are you all right sir?!" "I am not."replied Laven who was totally overburdened with woe. The landscape was beautiful with green grass, tall trees with extended canopies and merry birds. Laven could not find the dead bodies as they too disappeared along with that magical landscape cryptically created by God Nexus.

The squad now consisted of Laven, one elite warrior and two helpers only. They didn't have enough food or weapons and so the helpers went to search for eatables in and around the place. Laven sat disheartened in the carpet of grass sobbing upon the sacrifices he had to make in order to fulfil his moral duty. He lost his confidence and wanted to give up. He even ordered the team to pack up. The helpers brought a few fruits they could find without entering the deeper forest. The team started its journey back from the area where the Tower of Nexus was once situated to the point where the main road divided into two (as you might remember!).

Only a few hours had elapsed when one of the helpers heard the sound of a war horn far away. Laven ordered the helper to go ahead and spy out if the road was safe for journey or not. While Laven, elite and the other helper took shelter behind an old huge rock where they ate the

fruits and drank lots and lots of water. The spy detected enemy movements in the South and so he went from the South-east direction. After walking for a few more minutes, the spy saw a lot of dust in the air as if a huge army was marching towards their enemy kingdom. Very soon his theory turned into reality. Gabriel's most potent and professionally trained army was marching towards the Tower of Nexus. The spy ran like anything and informed Laven just in time. He said,"Your majesty, I can't believe my eyes. Never in my entire life I saw an army as huge and as professional as this one. They are marching in a very unique formation with their leader seated on a mythical elephant at the centre. The shield units are being followed up by the spears who in turn are followed up by the cavalry! Apart from this they have got giants, monsters and beasts of various sizes and shapes!
"Your majesty, how are we supposed to fight them that too without magic?"cried the other helper who by now was literally shivering with fear.

Laven got up from his place and took a deep breath of fresh air. He gathered the weapons and so that he only had his bow, a few arrows, a small sword and a knife. Each of the helpers had got their own knives and the elite had his influential sword and a bracelet with sharp pins attached to it. Once again the war horn was heard and this time quite near. "They will easily slaughter us or arrest us like this, we need to do something."cried the elite warrior who was ready for war and also prepared to die fighting for his master. The warrior's loyalty motivated Laven and Laven also gave a war cry. The sky was clear and wind was blowing pleasantly over the greenish landscape which was getting ready to drink the blood of dead warriors. Laven now heard the stamping of elephants, hooves of horses and footsteps of armoured fighters. Very soon this massive army appeared on the horizon and appeared in Laven's field of vision.

Nexus as you might remember didn't actually leave the place. He was sitting on his chariot which was well covered by the bushes. He wanted to enjoy a fight scene between humans. "Let's spectate the fighting skills of the King of the magical kingdom of Lavender,"he said to himself. But since Laven's side was weaker in terms of number, Nexus pulled out one of his hairs and threw it on the ground from which developed one hundred horsemen. The horsemen had swords with them and they charged towards the arriving army without waiting for any command either from Nexus or from Laven. Laven was surprised to see so many horsemen fighting for him that too all of a sudden. He asked the elite if he had used any magic to which the elite replied in negative. The horses jumped over the shield units and disoriented the infantry. However very soon they were all neutralised. Laven noticed that the leader of this army was a very fat general who could hardly move his body from one position to the other. He needed the help of three other men to get up and of a few more to walk. Nexus pulled out another hair and this time gave rise to five hundred boar riders. They too charged wildly without an order and clashed against the shield units. However they were effortlessly neutralised by the archers who were stationed behind the shield units. Nexus was assisting Laven because he didn't want Laven to die as Laven's fight with Gabriel was very essential for Astralyn to fight with her brother and this would neutralise any one of them and Morokar's Powers would collapse and Nexus could then easily get rid of Morokar. This time Nexus himself appeared in front of Laven as if he was there to protect Laven from the advancing army. The fat general was perplexed to see a God standing in front of mortal men and ordered his army to retreat but the army chiefs misunderstood his command and thought that they were asked to attack. The army chiefs shouted and encouraged their army to fight and within a fraction of seconds the whole army marched with double its speed towards Laven and God Nexus. Nexus hypnotised the shield units and elephants and made them fight among themselves. Then he took out his own sword and dashed towards the spears who were all annihilated in a few seconds. Laven also leaped upon the cavalry and killed most of the skilled horsemen. He harnessed a horse and charged towards the fat general. The fat general wanted to run but could not because of his extreme weight. Soon his neck was disconnected from his torso. The entire army was brought to its knees. And Nexus soon disappeared once again. Laven dismissed the army and got back to his expedition once again. Failing to understand as to why Nexus helped him, Laven kept on thinking about his future encounters in the Whispering Isles.

Whispers from the Whispering Isles

Fortunately Nexus left his divine chariot amidst the bushes. It was a brilliant copper chariot that was spotted in the dark hedges by one of the helpers of Laven. Laven, the elite warrior and the two helpers got up in the copper chariot and flew into the sky unlike any ordinary chariot. The two black horses were very beautiful and their vigour was very much like their owner, God Nexus.

Nature was serene in this part of the world and weather was very much good for a long journey. But the four men were very hungry and thirsty. They looked here and there in search of food and fresh water but found none. Laven was wondering about the might and diplomacy of Gods. Suddenly the team spotted something that was not at all anticipated. They saw six Royal Rages trying to block their air route. These Royal Rages as you might remember from the previous book were very ferocious and strong. They could burn down anything into ash. Soon the chariot was attacked by one of these Rages. Laven asked one of the helpers to manage the control of the horses and himself took to arms. While gaining victory over the huge army of the fat general, Laven and his squad gathered a lot of authoritative weapons that would allow them to fight concealed difficulties!

Laven showered a large number of arrows on the Rages. This did not make them fearful rather they got even more ferocious and violent. One Rage flew straight towards Laven and scratched his right upper thigh. Soon that region was bleeding profusely. One of the helpers tore a piece of cloth from his own clothing and bandaged that part.

Another Rage directly tried to slaughter the elite warrior but somehow he escaped. Soon a third Rage grabbed one of the helpers and ate him just in front of everyone. This scene was very disgusting and frightening for Laven and his team. Laven threw a long spear and slayed the Rage that was heading towards him. Laven ordered the helper to take the chariot in a different direction because the Rages would not allow them to go towards Whispering Isles.

The team finally landed over a low hill that was densely packed with forest and decided to spend that night there. The three of them were awfully tired, hungry and thirsty. No one was in a position to go and hunt for food. Laven didn't coerce them to do so. Soon it was pitch dark and the team somehow managed a fire. Laven heard the footsteps of something lurking in the deeper forest. He assumed it to be some animal and therefore went in the direction from which the sound was coming. The elite warrior followed his King but could not keep pace. Laven cleared off some of the branches with his sword and proceeded further. Thinking that he lost track of his master, the elite warrior returned back and told the helper about the sound that came from the deep forest. Soon both of them heard a loud cry of a male voice. They hurried towards that particular direction thinking that their master might be in some grave danger. But what they thought was false. Laven killed a muscular man with a thick black beard and a huge moustache. He was holding a primitive kind of sword and his dying red eyes were staring at Laven. Soon that man died and Laven came close to his team. He told them that this man was an assassin most probably sent by Gabriel to kill Laven!

Next morning the team spotted a creek that was a few yards below the hill. They also found some wild berries and tubers which they took as breakfast and started off their expedition towards Whispering Isles.

The sea was rough and so was the weather. Lightning and thunder made the journey difficult but not impossible. Laven realised that he was getting very late as a lot of time was wasted in the Tower of Nexus and so now he had to compensate for that time by travelling day and night. After two days of continuous journey the copper chariot abruptly disappeared and the team fell over a heap of sand. Everyone was perplexed. They roamed the place and it seemed like an island. The sea was very aggressive and it was raining heavily. A sense of unease washed over Laven and his team. The atmosphere was heavy and the whispers of the wind seemed to carry a foreboding message. The team made their way through a dense forest, following an old, overgrown path that led to a mansion.

Upon reaching the old mansion, they were greeted by the host, a man who introduced himself as Gabriel's uncle. He was tall, with an air of mystery about him, and his piercing gaze seemed to penetrate their very souls. The uncle said,"Welcome to this small group of isles. Very few and brave people actually visit us every year. They all come for different businesses. May I know for what reason you all are here?!"

Laven replied,"Myself Laven, the king of Lavender and I want to meet Gabriel, the king of this kingdom. We have got some loans to repay!"

"Ha ha ha, very funny! Kindly tell me clearly sir…why are you in this part of the world far from your own beautiful Lavender?!"asked the uncle.

The small group of isles was known for its eerie atmosphere and dark secrets that whispered through the winds. "Ok! Let's not bore you by asking questions. You may freshen yourselves up and get ready for lunch which is almost ready."said the uncle. "But sir, we have no gold to pay you for your service, we may help you out in work if any!"said Laven softly. "O my! No need to help me out my dear guest. I am your host and it's my duty to take utmost care of you, especially a king who has travelled so far for some unknown task or purpose. I would only request you to promise me that you and your team will join me on a game that we shall play after lunch. Is that ok for you?!"said the uncle.

Four men—Laven, The Elite warrior, the helper and Gabriel's uncle—found themselves drawn into the deadliest game they had ever encountered, "The Final Bet" ,promising unimaginable rewards but at an unfathomable cost.

With hearts pounding and adrenaline surging through their veins, the four made their way to a secluded, dimly lit cabin where the game was said to take place. As they entered the room, they were greeted by a shadowy figure known only as "The Dealer."

The Dealer explained the rules: each player would be given a unique weapon, and their objective was simple—be the last man standing. They would navigate through a maze-like arena filled with traps, obstacles, and hidden dangers, with the sole purpose of eliminating their opponents.

Laven and his team realised the gravity of the situation they were forced to enter. The walls of the maze closed behind them, sealing their fate within the deadly arena. Their camaraderie instantly shattered, replaced by a fierce determination to survive.

Laven, a skilled archer, received a sleek and deadly compound bow. The helper, an agile and quick thinker, was handed a pair of razor-sharp throwing knives. The Elite warrior held a menacing sledgehammer. And finally Uncle, a master of deception, was given a cloak of invisibility, rendering him nearly undetectable.

The game began, and the arena's eerie silence was shattered by the sounds of footsteps, weapon clashes, and echoing screams. Each one utilised their unique skills to navigate the labyrinth of death, searching for their opponents while avoiding lethal traps that lurked around every corner.

The tension mounted as Laven's arrow pierced through the darkness, striking the helper with deadly precision. Shocked and filled with a mix of remorse and survival instinct, Laven watched as the helper fell, gasping for breath. One down, three to go.

Uncle, cunning and elusive, utilised his cloak to stalk his prey silently. Shadows danced around him as he struck with lethal precision, eliminating the warrior with a swift, unexpected blow from behind. The sledgehammer fell, and the warrior's life was extinguished in an instant. Two down, two remained.

Laven and Gabriel's uncle, now pitted against each other, knew there could only be one survivor. With adrenaline coursing through their veins, they engaged in a deadly game of cat and mouse. Laven used his archery skills to unleash a flurry of arrows, while uncle cunningly evaded each deadly shot, relying on his cloak to remain hidden.

As the minutes turned into hours, fatigue and desperation began to cloud their judgement. They were consumed by a relentless desire to be the one who emerged victorious, leaving the other as a lifeless body on the cold, unforgiving floor.

Finally, in a heart-pounding moment of reckoning, Laven's arrow found its mark, piercing Uncle's heart. The cloak of invisibility slipped away as uncle crumpled to the ground, his life extinguished. In that haunting silence, Laven stood alone as the last man standing.

But as the dust settled and the reality of what had transpired sunk in, a chilling realisation gripped Laven's soul. The once vibrant friendship they had shared had been shattered, replaced by a trail of bodies and broken trust. The thrill of victory was overshadowed by the haunting memories of the lives lost and the darkness they had succumbed to.

Leaving the cabin, Laven vowed to honour the memories of his fallen friends.

The Ricochet of Destiny

Laven earned his life by killing Gabriel's uncle. He was alone now and was feeling very lonely. A heavy sadness burdened his soft heart and didn't allow it to expand at its own free will. The atmosphere was gloomy and the Sun was far far away from this part of the world. The currents in the sea were as uneven as mountains stretched over a huge stretch of land. The wind was eerie and Laven slowly walked along the meadowing lane to reach the end of this world as he was imagining in his mind. Finally a point came when Laven had neutralised all traps and hitches set for him by Gabriel and now was in a position to rescue Piper from the hands of this seductive devil. He was shown the path to the Castle in which Piper was on house arrest. The Castle was situated on an island which was the smallest amongst all the isles of the Whispering Isles. Laven made a raft out of bamboo that was available in the forest and used it to reach his destination island.

The journey through the rough sea was not at all easy and the sea as I already mentioned was very very jagged. Soon it rained cats and dogs and Laven landed on an island which was not supposed to be his terminus. Laven was shown the direction by a golden light that accompanied him like a loyal pet. The island on which Laven was compelled to land by nature had a mystery of its own. Since it was a very small island Laven unveiled the mystery by discovering a unique disc which was luminous. It had something written on it but was not readable due to the intense light it emitted. It was no doubt hot but Laven held it with the help of two big leaves.

It so happened that Laven was trying to figure out more about the disc when someone hit him on his head from behind. A silence prevailed throughout the island and the shadow of Laven slowly disappeared as he was lifted and carried by someone who could fly. Laven opened his eyes and found himself inside a castle. He got up on his knees and saw royal furniture in and around the place. He now got up on his legs and moved around trying to figure out where he was and who was that evil spirit that brought him here. He again spotted the golden light outside a small royal window. He dashed towards it and flung it open. The golden light moved inside and had a total gyration once around the place and moved out of the window again. Laven also jumped out of the window as the room where he was lying was not at much height from the ground. The golden light once again directed Laven to a storeroom which was crammed with a variety of weapons. Laven picked up a bow, a few arrows, a spear, a shield and a small sword. He was now fully equipped for a duel. A duel that would decide the future of Piper Forest who was very frail and was under the burden of diseases. She was weeping by the side of the only window that opened from her room. It was the only connection between her and the outside world. Piper was used as a commodity of pleasure by that seductive Gabriel.

Laven could now hear the lamentation of Piper. A sense of consummation erupted in Laven's face. His ears were longing for the voice of Piper from such a protracted period of time and now wanted to perceive it at least for some more time. Laven stood there frozen for a few minutes. His senses were slowly coming out of their dormant phase and suddenly there was a burst of energy in him. He was ready to do anything to get her out. He tracked the sound and soon reached the same window beside which Piper was weeping. Now they were in a position in which only the windowpane stood between them. Piper let Laven enter the room by opening the window in utter excitement. She always had faith in this boy. A mixture of anticipation, nostalgia, relief, curiosity and connection ran through Piper's spine! With an increasing libido, Laven became more attuned to his senses.

A Clash of Magic and Steel

The door of Piper's room flung open and there was a boy owning striking features that made him both alluring and intimidating. Standing at an average height for his age, his confident posture and commanding presence gave him an air of authority that belies his youthful appearance. His face is defined by chiselled features, flawlessly symmetrical and carved with precision. His skin is faultless, seemingly untouched by blemishes, lending him an almost ethereal quality. His eyes are enchanting, the windows to a mind filled with ambition and sly plans. They are a mesmerising shade of deep, penetrating green, framed by thick, dark lashes that enhance their intensity. He smoothly draws people into his web of manipulation, leaving them spellbound by his charisma and unaware of the darkness that lies beneath.

Inside the grand castle's opulent halls, an epic battle unfolded, pitting Laven against the nefarious villain. The atmosphere was charged with tension as the clash of steel echoed through the ancient stone walls, punctuated by bursts of arcane energy and deafening roars.

Laven, adorned in gleaming armour, possessed a righteous fury in his eyes, fuelled by his firm determination to protect the innocent and vanquish evil. He brandished a mighty sword, its blade shimmering with an otherworldly light, as he relentlessly advanced upon the villain.

Gabriel, draped in dark robes that seemed to absorb light itself, exuded an air of nastiness. His piercing gaze bore the mark of a twisted mind, and he wielded dark magic with petrifying expertise. Waves of shadowy energy cascaded from his fingertips, clashing against Laven's defences.

As the confrontation escalated, they carved their path through the castle, crushing intricate tapestries and toppling priceless statues in their wake. Sparks flew as the Laven's sword clashed against Gabriel's mystical shield, each strike resonating with the weight of their convictions.

Laven's valour surged, driving him forward, determined to end Gabriel's reign of trepidation and darkness. With a swift manoeuvre, he disarmed his adversary, sending Gabriel's staff flying across the space. But Gabriel was not so easily defeated. He retaliated with an ambush of dark spells, coercing Laven to summon his inner strength to guard himself from the onslaught.

Their conflict spilled out onto the castle's battlements, high above the crashing waves of the sea below. As the wind whipped through their hair, they continued their furious dance of combat. Laven's sword and Gabriel's dark magic clashed in a breath-taking display of power and dexterity.

The Guardian's Scrutiny

A storm began to brew, mirroring the tempest within their battle. Lightning illuminated the darkened skies, casting an eerie glow on their tussle. Laven, drawing upon the energy of the elements, launched a devastating counterattack, his strikes imbued with elemental fury.

Realising he was outmatched, the villain summoned his last reserves of strength, conjuring a vortex of darkness. The swirling void threatened to engulf Laven. Zephyrus was summoned from Heaven by Gabriel. Zephyrus entered into Gabriel's physical body and started to manipulate Gabriel's mind, body and soul.

Soon that golden light that guided Laven reappeared and transformed into an aura of descending light from Heaven. Dark clouds roofed the sky. Wind speed increased by several fold and Laven could feel the vibrations of divine entities. A bright golden light fell on the rocky shore. Astralyn adorned in resplendent golden armour was descending from Heaven. Her very presence commands attention and reverence. She is the embodiment of strength, wisdom and unwavering resolve.

Across her chest, a breastplate guards her heart, a shining emblem of invincibility. Expertly forged, it bears intricate engravings that depict epic tales of valour and triumph. Golden pauldrons protect her shoulders, each etched with symbols that epitomise the forces of creation and destruction she wields.

In her left hand, she brandishes a mighty shield, also adorned with golden embellishments. It is a formidable defence, revealing the symbol of a blazing sun at its centre. The shield serves as a bulwark against evil and chaos, its radiant aura instilling audacity and faith in all who stand in its presence.

In her right hand, she wields a gleaming spear, an extension of her divine authority. The spearhead, forged from celestial metals, blazes with an ethereal glow. Its intricate designs depict constellations and cosmic forces, embodying her mastery over the cosmic realms. With this spear, she strikes down injustice, enforces divine justice, and safeguards the balance of the universe.

As this powerful goddess stands tall, radiating strength and grace, her golden armour, shield, and spear symbolise her indomitable spirit and her dedication to safeguarding the cosmos. She is a beacon of light and empowerment, a celestial force that inspires mortals and gods alike, forever etching her name in the annals of divine legends.

As the sun began to set, casting an ethereal golden glow over the hostile sea shore, a fierce battle was about to unfold. Standing amidst the crumbling pillars was the female goddess, a figure emanating divine radiance and strength. Her eyes sparkled with determination as she prepared to face her adversary. An astonished Laven stood behind Astralyn.

Across from her, a human villain, Gabriel, once a mere mortal, now under the nefarious control of a malevolent devil. His features were twisted, reflecting the darkness that consumed his soul. Veins pulsed with otherworldly power, enhancing his physical abilities to superhuman levels. Hatred burned in his eyes as he eagerly awaited the opportunity to strike down the goddess.

The tension in the air was palpable as the goddess, adorned in flowing robes and a crown of celestial light, extended her hand. A brilliant beam of energy erupted from her palm, crackling with divine power. The attack surged toward the villain, who smirked and raised his arm, his flesh now covered in spooky, blackened armour.

With a sinister laugh, Gabriel deflected the goddess's assault effortlessly. The energy dissipated into the air, creating a spectacular display of light. He lunged forward, his movements impossibly quick, striking at the goddess with a series of lightning-fast blows. Each strike carried a malevolent force, propelled by the devil's influence.

However, the goddess was not so easily vanquished. She gracefully dodged the villain's attacks, her movements fluid and precise. As he swung a wickedly sharp sword, she spun away, the air shimmering around her as a shield of divine energy formed to protect her. Her hands began to glow with an otherworldly aura, channelling the immense power she commanded.

In an instant, she unleashed a counterattack, releasing a torrent of elemental forces. Flames danced around her fingertips, gusts of wind howled around her, and waves surged forth from her palms. The elements converged into a swirling storm, aimed directly at the devil. The tempest crashed into him, its intensity causing the ground to shake and debris to fly.

Yet, even amidst the chaos, the villain remained defiant. With an incantation whispered in a devilish tongue, he summoned dark energies to bolster his strength. His eyes turned a menacing shade of crimson as he charged forward, shrugging off the elemental offensive.

Their clash continued, a dance of light and shadow, as the goddess and villain exchanged powerful strikes and evasive manoeuvres. The shore trembled with the sheer force of their confrontation, the air filled with the clash of their powers.

But the goddess's determination never wavered. She drew upon her divine essence, her very essence entwined with the forces of creation. With one final surge of strength, she unleashed a devastating burst of pure energy, blinding in its brilliance. The villain's form was engulfed, his malevolent energy ripped away, leaving him nothing more than a shattered shell.

As the battle concluded, the goddess stood amidst the debris, her regal figure shining with triumph. Her eyes, a reflection of the heavens, surveyed the aftermath of the conflict. She had prevailed against the human villain controlled by the devil's sway, once again affirming the indomitable power of the divine against the forces of darkness. As Astralyn annihilated her brother Zephyrus just before Aurora's feather touched the floor, Morokar fell on his knees. His hopes and aspirations shattered. He lost all of his divine clouts and now was very livid at Astralyn. Nexus softly entered Morokar's room and stabbed him on his back with a sharp blade. Very soon Morokar's body disintegrated into millions of tiny particles and fell over Astralyn. The sea shore was restored into its original beauty when Astralyn died out into thin air.

The Psychic Rift

Piper came running towards Laven who stood tall beside the absolutely destroyed body of Gabriel. Piper held Laven by his arm and persuaded him to take her away from this place at once as she could not bear to see any more bloodshed.

The golden light was now no more and Laven was lost along with Piper in one of the islands of the Whispering Isles.
Laven and Piper stood together on the moonlit cliff overlooking a gigantic, tranquil sea. The reverberations of their recent struggle against evil still resounded through the air, but in this moment, they found solace in each other's presence. The moon bathed them in a soft glow, casting a romantic ambiance around them.

Piper, her hazel eyes filled with appreciation and admiration, looked up at Laven. She couldn't help but be captivated by the strength and gallantry he had exhibited while fronting the seductive devil, Gabriel. Laven, his heart still racing from the intense battle, returned her gaze, his eyes reflecting a mixture of relief and affection.

As they stood there, the wind gently tousled Piper's chestnut locks, causing them to dance around her face.

Laven reached out, inept to resist the urge to tuck a loose strand behind her ear. His touch sent a shiver down her spine, and a blush crept onto her cheeks.

"Laven," Piper spoke softly, her voice carrying a hint of vulnerability. "I don't know what I would have done without you. You saved me from that seductive devil, Gabriel. You risked your life for me."

Laven's hand slightly cupped Piper's cheek, his thumb caressing her skin tenderly. His voice was filled with sincerity as he replied, "Piper, I would go to the ends of the earth and beyond to protect you. You mean more to me than anything in this world. No devil, no matter how seductive, could ever come between us."

A warm smile blossomed on Piper's face, her eyes sparkling with affection. She placed her hand atop Laven's, revelling in the strength of their connection. The weight of their shared experiences drew them closer together, forming an unbreakable bond.

Leaning in, Laven pressed his lips gently against Piper's, their first kiss a testament to the triumph over darkness and the birth of something lovely. In that moment, time seemed to stand still as their hearts beat in harmony, their souls entwining.

They pulled apart, their eyes locked in an intimate gaze, conveying a wealth of unspoken emotions. Laven's arms enveloped Piper in a protective embrace, drawing her close to his chest. As they held each other, the world faded away, leaving only the two of them and the promise of a future filled with love, adventure, and the strength to conquer any challenge that may come their way.

Together, Laven and Piper stood on that moonlit cliff, their hearts entwined, ready to face whatever lay ahead, knowing that their love was unbending and their bond indestructible.

The Ultimate Fate

A sudden thought struck the vaguest corner of Laven's mind. The thought was about the disc. Yes, the magical disc that was emitting a lot of light. He shared it with Piper and she also got curious about the same. The duo walked across the rocky coast towards the castle which was nothing more than a horrific prison that tested her patient and tolerance. After having a nutritious meal at the castle's elegant dining hall which was once used by Gabriel. The dining table was profusely decorated with gold artefacts and the chairs were so comfortable that after sitting on them every other chair would be uncomfortable! The silver utensils and copper candelabras were also very striking apart from the state of the art architecture of the hall.

After their meal the couple moved back to the shore and Laven recovered a small raft that was poorly hidden and roofed by a creeper. The couple sailed with the help of the raft and started their hunt for the island with the disc. After three unsuccessful attempts Laven finally stopped his raft as their prey was just in front. Laven recognised the place at once and took his steps carefully and cautiously towards the location where the disc was spotted for the first time by him. Piper following Laven reached a place that was just beneath a huge hemlock tree. Laven threw his hand towards the disc that was lying in a very awkward position. He tried to observe it acutely thinking that it had something critical which its maker wanted the discoverer to know. Piper, whose curiosity was now breaking all limits, persuaded her lover to give that disc to her. Little did she realise that this disc was much more heftier than what it seemed. The disc spontaneously fell from Piper's weak hands and hit the ground disintegrating into two equal pieces. It so happened that the surroundings radically changed. Laven suddenly felt as if his magical powers had returned. Laven tried to cast a healing spell on himself and Piper and it worked! The restrictions on magical powers were lifted as it was this very disc designed by the finest wizard which was responsible for the magic line and its effects over the space inside it. With the help of his magic and profound concentration Laven summoned his magical chariot and the couple quickly got over it.

Soon Laven and Piper found themselves in the village of Felix. Its condition severely improved and its inhabitants were living peacefully and happily far away from misery and distress. What never changed was the wind and temperature of the place. Laven was warmly welcomed by the villagers and everyone congratulated the couple. After spending a beautiful night in the most peaceful hut of the village, the couple continued towards Lavender.

After a long and tiresome journey they finally reached the magical defence wall of Lavender which was commissioned by Laven during his reign!

'During his reign!' Yes, Lavender now was no longer under the control of Laven. Its king was a teenager who was the only son of a minister of the royal council. After a long and nasty negotiation the couple was allowed to enter Lavender! Laven decided to stay with Piper in a very small village on the outskirts of Lavender. Soon the news of

Laven's arrival spread like wildfire and people came in hundreds to meet and greet their beloved king (former king).

The council was apprehensive of Laven's presence in Lavender and deliberated on it with the teen king.

Finally one fine day a minister arrived at Laven's place and greeted Laven. He was tall and thin and was dressed in a white attire which had a golden lining. His face was glowing and his smile was piercing.

He said,"Laven Warlock, the council is exultant to find you and your beloved in good mind and body. We already lost confidence in you and so the next king was appointed in haste. But still our king is performing his duty diligently and is not out of the kingdom running after self-seeking motives. His love towards his kingdom has surpassed all limits and so we are all very happy under his regime."

Laven responded,"I didn't leave my kingdom to deteriorate, for I had discussed my actions with the council several times and it was only after continual consultation that I had finally decided to undertake the expedition. I am very unhappy with the way the council treated me even after knowing everything I contributed during my regime. I want my position back and tell your teen king that I challenge..." "No no please, don't go with a challenge. He is only seventeen and you are a robust muscular man. It goes against the rules of the council."interrupted the cunning minister.

Laven didn't speak out anything and looked out of the muddy window into the vast stretch of Lavender coloured flowers that were boogying in the wind and laughing at the Sun. The Sun was doomed to see the flowers laughing at him but could not do anything as they were covered by a kaleidoscope of innocent butterflies. Laven could relate it with his condition!

The minister cried,"In order to not disappoint you the council has summoned you to the royal palace where you shall be given a chance to put forward your points and if found adequate, your opinion will be taken into account!" Saying this the minister quickly left the place not even bothering to wait for a response. His assertiveness was not acceptable and his rough way of putting things dug several holes in Laven's broad heart.

Laven gave the invitation a second thought and ultimately decided to go towards the royal palace.

Piper was overhearing their conversation and was hiding behind the curtain.

In the royal palace, the windows gave passage to the cool breeze and the smell of elegantly coloured flowers. Motivational music was heard in and around the premises of the planning complex. Laven moved into the meeting room which had an enormous table on which Laven once discussed policies with his ministers. Now the table was engaged with new faces and Laven sat on a chair which was just opposite to the chair of the king where the teen sat. On his right was the person who visited Laven and to his left was a fat person, maybe the king's advisor. On Laven's right was a minister with a thick moustache and long beard and to his left was a thin and middle aged minister. They introduced themselves to Laven and grinned at his blank face. Soon after this, the conversations began and the teen king introduced Laven to everyone present in the hall. The door to the hall was just behind Laven's chair and it was kept open. There were a few strong guards outside the room but none was allowed inside for some spy might take unlawful advantage. After a protracted speech delivered by the king and one minister, Laven was allowed to speak out. It was just when Laven opened his mouth to speak out his very first word when the person on his right stabbed him in his abdomen a bit towards the right of the umbilicus. Before Laven could get up from his chair, a subsequent attack landed on his left thigh near the groin. Laven bellowed like anything. A third attack came right on his back from a guard who entered the room and thrusted his long spear through and through Laven's body. By this time Laven had already got up from his seat and gripped the chair on which he was sitting. He held it tightly and swung it to hit the head of the person behind him. The person behind him fell unconscious on the floor with such a heavy blow and was bleeding profusely. Laven quickly turned his head towards the king and saw that the teen was laughing like anything. He then looked down at the unconscious person on the floor and was in grave shock! It was Piper who was bleeding profusely. Laven hit her on her head and almost killed her. The other ministers also laughed out loudly and soon the entire hall was laughing at Laven and his dying friend. Laven already lost a lot of blood and was barely surviving. The king came close to his neck and whispered in his right ear,"we abducted Piper when you left her alone in that poor hut! And now that you have killed her yourself you ought not to survive." Saying this the teen stabbed Laven in his right carotid triangle and soon Laven's dead body freely fell on the floor with a thud. The king came close to Laven's dead body and humiliated it by kicking it and pressing its chest with his strong and tall boots. He asked the house if it was happy with the kind of punishment

Laven received to which the house replied in unison,"He didn't deserve such easy death!!" The King asked the guards to take the dead bodies away and he himself left the hall at once.

The king went to his royal bedroom which once belonged to Laven and sat over the edge of the large comfortable bed. He was looking here and there when something was spotted by him outside the window. It seemed like a red mat that was hanging or flying outside beckoning him...